Gas

the chef

by

Michael Little

ISBN No: 1 903172 63 2

Publishers: Barny Books
              Hough on the Hill,
              Grantham,
              Lincolnshire,
              NG32 2BB

              Tel: 01400 250246
              Email: Barnybooks@hotmail.co.uk

For Margot, my granddaughter
and all young at heart readers
whatever their age.

Gaston makes a bad career move

It had been a busy day at the Sacrebleu restaurant and the chef, Gaston Renouille was resting in his armchair when his smallest grandchild said, "Tell us about when you were young, Grandpapa."

"Alors, cher têtard, I was not always a chef. In my youth I wanted to be an artist and be famous for painting beautiful pictures."

"Tell us what happened Grandpapa?"

Gaston took a sip of wine and started to talk.

Gaston loved to tell stories
and some of them were true.

Try these for size, sonny

"The family Renouille have always been chefs. When I was old enough to lose my tail, my father said to me, 'Now you must go to Paris to become a chef and here is your first pair of chef's trousers'."

I was very excited to be leaving home and going to work in the big city where I might make new friends and have a good time.

My father wrote a letter of introduction *'To whom it may concern'*.

It read: *'The bearer of this letter is my son, Gaston, a good lad and a hard worker who has been brought up to respect food. He eats anything, and will be a great help to you in the restaurant business. Please give him a job. You won't regret it.*

Your obedient servant,
Goulache Renouille.

Armed with this generous recommendation and eager to start my new life, I arrived in the big city. I was amazed at the number of restaurants which I found on every boulevard, alley and street.

I offered myself and my letter of introduction to the managers of cafés, bistros, smart dining rooms and, even low dives but none of them wanted a country frog. Finally, worn out with tramping the streets and, on the point of giving up, my luck changed.

The head chef of a seedy-looking restaurant named the Zut Alors in an unfashionable district was on the look out for a replacement for a kitchen assistant whom he had fired for asking for a pay rise. He took me on with the promise of food but no wages. I was thrilled by this handsome offer and flattered by his confidence in me. I lost no time in proving my worth.

I made a lot of mistakes to begin with.

Recipes for disaster

But I also had a lot of fun when the boss wasn't looking.

Life in a busy Parisian restaurant was very hard so it was a great treat when my fellow chefs suggested a picnic in the park on our day off. That was where I became very friendly with Gigi, an artists' model who told me all about the wonderful life artists lead.

She described the all-night parties, the excited discussions about art and music, the amusing clothes or lack of clothes, the freedom to be untidy and the glamorous exhibition opening nights. Artists, she said, were admired and envied for their unconventional lifestyles by ordinary people who led dull, conventional lives, and who only concerned themselves with making money.

Gigi's words excited me so much that I decided to stop cooking at once and become an artist.

I quit my job at the Zut Alors and, having scrounged some money from my new friends, I bought paint, brushes, canvases, an easel, a beret, and all the other paraphernalia essential to the rôle of artist.

With my heart pounding with excitement I purchased a map of the world and started to plan my escape into my new life.

Trouble in paradise

I hadn't realised that there were so many countries in the world or that so many of them had dangerously foreign sounding names in languages I felt sure I wouldn't understand. At last I found what I was looking for. It was warm. It was cheap. It was beautiful.

It was Martinique.

I bought myself a one-way ticket and, the next day, I was on my way to the tropical paradise of Martinique where, surrounded by palm trees and beautiful girls I would be inspired to paint unforgettable pictures and thus, make my fortune.

My plan was to paint 100 pictures and return to Paris where I would have a wildly successful exhibition, sell all my pictures and become rich and famous. Gigi had told me that even a country frog from a humble pond could meet all the greatest people in the land and be admired by them if he was a successful artist.

I couldn't wait to get started.

When I arrived in Martinique, I settled in nicely in Little Krak, a village in a delightful swamp in the shade of a smoky mountain, and started painting immediately. The scenery was wonderful, it rained twice a day and the air was full of the most delicious insects.

All I had to do was hold out my plate, and in a moment it was filled with the most tempting butterflies and bugs of all kinds. I had so much to eat I was in danger of getting fat and lazy.

It was paradise.

I settled in nicely in Little Krak

The only problem was that it got noisy at night with all the singing coming from the next village, Great Krak. I paddled over one night to see what was going on and entered a bar where the locals were having their choir practice. Some of the words of the songs would make you blush so I won't tell you them.

I chatted to a frog with a fine tenor croak who told me his name was Gogo, and guess what? He was a fellow artist from Paris! Small world, eh? He promised to give me painting tips in return for drinks at the bar.

Suddenly the room went quiet

While I was ordering a round of drinks, my eye was caught by a curious old faded picture of a most horrible monster on the wall behind the bar. I enquired the name of this nasty piece of work, and suddenly the room went quiet and the choir began to speak in whispers.

"What's up?" said I.

"You mustn't speak its name or it will bring bad luck on the village," I was told.

Gogo then explained that the evil one was a monster crab named Krepitus which lived in the sea and came out at night to gobble up unfortunate frogs. This is why the frogs of Great Krak sing all night long to stop them being afraid. The crab is supposed to be hundreds of years old. All attempts to capture and kill him have failed.

"We must do something to help." said Gogo and, together, we hatched up a Great Scheme.

14

How to kill a monster

The next day Gogo and I put up a big sign on the shore near where Krepitus came out at night. The sign read:

BE FAMOUS! BE THE ENVY OF THE WORLD!
Have your portrait painted by a great Frog artist from Paris
Big discounts for crabs.
Ring the bell for attention

And we hung up a bell on a tree and waited for nightfall. We were scared, hiding in the bushes, listening to the faint sound of the choir in Great Krak and wishing we were at home in our cosy swamp.

Then, around midnight, there was a great bubbling and frothing in the sea and out crawled Krepitus, the monster crab, looking mean and waving his claws.

His eyes stood out on stalks when he saw our sign

His eyes stood out on stalks when he saw our sign. He scratched his head with a claw as he slowly read the message. We could see he was interested. Then, making up his mind, he gave the bell an almighty tug.

The distant choir fell silent, and Gogo and I stepped out of the shadows.

"Yes, can I help you?" said Gogo in an insolent tone.

The monster Krepitus looked at us for a moment and said in a bubbling, hissing voice, "Which one of you is the Frog artist?"

"C'est moi, Maître Gogo," announced Gogo grandly, "what can I do for you?"

"Can you really make me famous?" hissed the vain monster.

"Bien sûr!" Gogo replied, "make an appointment with my assistant, Gaston."

We arranged that Krepitus should come to sit for his portrait the following day by the shores of the Black Lagoon, which we told him was a local beauty spot. This was untrue. The Black Lagoon was a lake of thick sticky goo which swallowed everything that fell into it. Nothing could survive falling into the Black Lagoon.

Gogo and I set up an easel on the bank of the Black Lagoon and prepared a large canvas with an impressive frame. We waited. Krepitus was late for his appointment, just to show us how important he was. He had dressed up for the occasion in a purple cloak with oyster shell buttons. He looked a right prawn but Gogo complimented him on his fine turn out.

"Where shall I stand?" hissed the crab.

"My assistant will assist you," said Gogo suavely, squeezing out blobs of paint onto his palette.

I directed Krepitus to stand on the bank with his back to the lagoon. "Magnifique!" said Gogo, "What a profile, such nobility, what a fine head, just step back a little, monsieur."

"How's this?" asked Krepitus, putting his body into reverse gear and edging towards the bank.

"I can't get you in the frame, monsieur, just a little further away if you please" said Gogo. And then the monster lost his footing. With a terrible croaking roar he plunged backwards into the Black Lagoon. He raved and hissed and waved his claws about but all his efforts only made him sink further into the black sticky goo. His eyes on stalks were the last things to go and I'll never forget the evil look he gave us as the Lagoon swallowed him up.

Needless to say, we were heroes. The villagers of Great Krak put on an enormous party for us and we sang happily till dawn.

A painting lesson interrupted

We had gone out, Gogo and I, for a day's painting, and had set up our easels with a good view of the smoky mountain, and started work. After some hours, when I was feeling quite pleased with my achievement, Gogo sauntered over to give me some good advice.

Gogo was one of these artists who is never content with things as they are. He must make improvements on nature's handiwork and he was forever urging me to throw away my black paint and only use bright colours. On this occasion we nearly came to blows because of his insistence on my using the wrong colours when painting landscape.

19

We were standing in front of a green palm tree with a grey trunk at the time, and Gogo started shouting at me, "Orange leaves, purple trunk, you imbecile!"

I retorted,"Any fool can see it is a grey trunk."

"Calling me a fool, are you?" he snarled, turning nasty and waving a palette knife.

"Right " said I, "what colour do you call that then?" pointing to an enormous cloud of black smoke emerging from the mountain in front of us.

It began to rain rocks

Before he could say something daft like "purple" there was a deafening explosion from the mountain and it began to rain rocks.

We dived for cover as red-hot (or as Gogo would say, orangey-purply violet) boulders rained down on us.

Steam was coming out of the swamp. The Black Lagoon burst into flames. It looked like the villages of Little and Great Krak would be covered in hot ash. My only thought was to rescue my paintings from the studio and get away as fast as I could.

Dodging the burning missiles we raced for our studios. Grabbing up armfuls of our precious canvases, we headed for the sea in a desperate attempt to outrace the fires which were now spreading over the island, fanned by a sudden vicious wind.

21

Together, Gogo and I hurriedly packed our belongings into a small boat and paddled frantically out to sea. Even there we were not safe. The black cloud of smoke descended upon us and we were in danger of losing our way, if we knew which way that was.

All the time Gogo was muttering, "Purple, greenish-brown, yellowy-lime."

I didn't wish to provoke him, as he clearly was in a bad mood, nature having spoiled his colour scheme. I paddled on in silence until we were clear of the island. We survived on midges and the little worms which were eating the planks of our boat.

Sighting land on the third day, we made for the shore and Gogo hopped out.

"Green, Ha Ha!" they exclaimed rudely

A crowd of curious natives surrounded us and started pointing at our skin and shouting, "Green, ha! ha!" Gogo went purple with rage and immediately started an argument about nature getting colours all wrong and what they were seeing wasn't green; it was just that they were looking at it the wrong way.

They pretended to agree with Gogo because they were scared of him and started to say the opposite of the truth. This led to much confusion. Husbands would scold their wives for serving grey midge cake for dinner when it should be rosy-violet with pink flecks. Wives would compliment their husbands on their colourful language when they'd had one too many at the bar.

It all got a bit too much for me so I packed up the boat. One night I paddled away leaving Gogo trying to convince these native brown frogs that they were purple, yellow, bluish-violet, orangey-beige, crimson, vermilion, gamboge, Naples yellow, ultramarine blue, heliotrope, magenta etc., but not brown.

23

I was determined to get back home

I was spotted by a passing steamer after some days and taken on board on condition I worked my passage home by helping the cook in his kitchen, and by painting portraits of the captain and his crew, a rough and villainous looking lot. They were, however, very pleased with their portraits, and promised to have copies tattooed on themselves as soon as the ship docked in N'wawlins.

A shock awaited me on my return to Paris. Fashions had changed while I was away in Martinique and nobody wanted to look at my paintings.

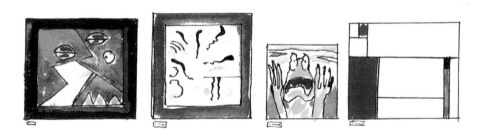

I was disappointed to find myself out of fashion, and try as I would, I could not make any sense of the paintings I saw in the galleries. Nor could I understand the people who raved about them. It seemed that all my hard work in far off Martinique was wasted.

In a state of utter dejection I hauled my cartload of paintings around to the Zut Alors and, ordering a mint tea, I pondered what to do next.

To cheer myself up, I called on my friend, Gigi, and recounted to her all my adventures. She was very pleased to see me, and had kind words to say about my paintings but thought I was more suited to a life of cooking. She even offered to give up being an artists' model and marry me if I would settle down and open a restaurant.

My reaction to her thrilling proposal was, "Sacrebleu! Gigi, you're right, I'll do it!"

"That's not a bad name for a restaurant. We'll call it the Sacrebleu!" she said.

Sacrebleu!

"I like it." I said.

And what happened to Gogo?

The last I saw of him was on the island of the brown frogs, teaching them to like bright colours.

He must have had some success, judging from the photo he sent me.

Family album

Goulache Renouille

Madame Galette Renouille

Menu du Jour

Chef Gaston Renouille recommends

Watercress and Midge soup
Pâté de Woodlouse
Worm farci

Gnat Compote
Papillon en Daube
Crapaud en Trou

Papillotte de Papillon
Cuckoospit Meringue
Mosquito Sorbet

All mains served with a side order of
Duckweed Sauté

Bon Appétit

Sacrebleu!

The End